The Little Mermaid

Illustrated by Eric Kincaid

SHOOTING STAR PRESS

The King of the Sea and his family live in a palace on the seabed. Fish swim in and out of the palace all the time. The King's family have tails like the fish.

The King's daughters
are the mermaids.
They find things
from shipwrecks.
They put them
in their gardens.
One little mermaid
has a statue of
a boy in her
garden.

Her grandmother
tells her stories.
The little mermaid
likes stories
about people.

When mermaids grow up they can go
to the surface of the sea. This is
the first time the little mermaid
has been to the surface. The sea
is shiny and flat, like glass.
She can see a ship.

There is a prince
on the ship. He is
like the statue
of the boy in
her garden.

The wind begins to blow. There is
a storm coming. It starts to rain.
The ship is tossed by the waves.
Suddenly the ship turns over. It
is sinking. The prince is thrown
into the water. He is drowning.

The little mermaid does not want the prince to drown. She puts her arms round him. She stops him sinking. The waves take them to the shore. The little mermaid lays the prince on the sand. His eyes are closed but he is alive.

There is someone
coming. The little
mermaid hides
behind a rock. She
sees some girls.
The girls see the prince. They do
not see the little mermaid. They
carry the prince away.

The little mermaid goes home to the palace under the sea. She sits in her garden and looks at the statue of the boy. She thinks about the prince all the time.

Her mermaid sisters find out where the prince is living. They take the little mermaid to the place.

The little mermaid visits the bay every night. She watches the prince. She cannot go to him because she cannot walk. She has no feet. Every night she is more sad. "I will ask the witch to change my tail into legs and feet," she says. "Then perhaps the prince will love me."

"I will help if you give me your
voice," says the witch. The little
mermaid loves to sing but she loves
the prince more. "You will die
if the prince ever loves another
better than you!" warns the witch.

"Please do as I ask," says the little mermaid. The witch mixes her a potion.

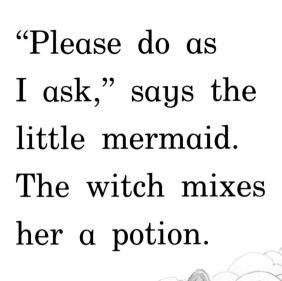

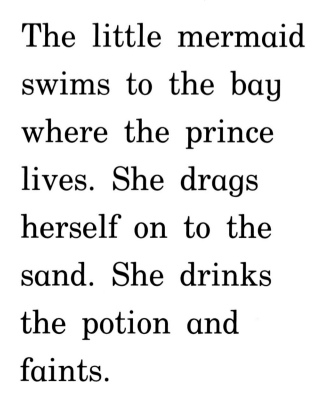

The little mermaid swims to the bay where the prince lives. She drags herself on to the sand. She drinks the potion and faints.

When the little
mermaid opens her
eyes, the prince
is standing beside
her. "Who are
you?" he asks.
"Where have you
come from?"
She cannot answer
because she has
no voice.
The prince takes
her to his palace.
Her new feet hurt
with every step
she takes.

The little mermaid dances gracefully. Nobody knows how much her new feet hurt.

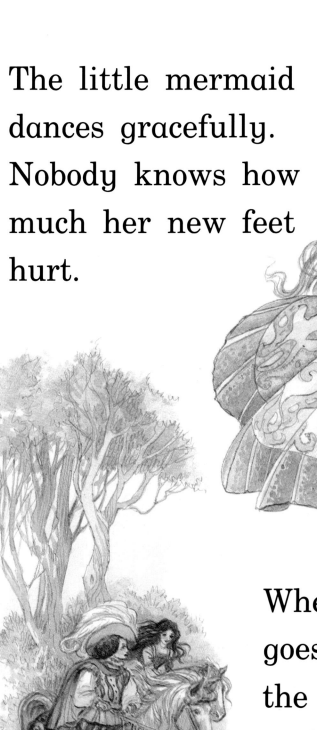

When the prince goes riding, he takes the little mermaid with him. At night she sleeps on a velvet cushion outside his door.

One night, when everyone is asleep, she goes to bathe her feet in the sea. Her sisters come to see her. They tell her they miss her. Her father and her grandmother are missing her too. They wave to her from some way off.

The prince grows to
love the little
mermaid like a
sister. She is
very happy. Then,
one day, the King
sends the prince
to see a princess.
The prince does not
want to go. The
King says he must.

As soon as the prince sees the
princess he wants to marry her.
The little mermaid remembers what
the witch said. She is very sad.
She knows she will die. On the day
of the wedding everyone is happy,
except for the little mermaid.

After the wedding they go on board a ship. The little mermaid's sisters follow the ship. They have cut off their long hair. "We have found a way to save you," they call to the little mermaid. "We have given the witch our hair. In return she has given us a knife which will break the spell."

Then the sisters shout to the little mermaid, "You must kill the prince. His blood must fall on your feet. Then your feet will turn back into a tail. You will be a mermaid again and you can come back to our palace under the sea."

The little mermaid looks at the sleeping prince. She cannot harm him. She would rather die herself. The little mermaid throws the knife into the sea. Then she throws herself into the sea. She changes into sparkling foam and is never seen again.

All these appear in the pages of the story. Can you find them?

King of the Sea

mermaid

statue

ship